For Annabelle—E. A.

For Tristan and Keira, my favorite mad-scientists-in-training—B. A.

Published by Charlesbridge
85 Main Street, Watertown, MA 02472
(617) 926-0329 · www.charlesbridge.com

Illustrations done in ink with color washes and assembled digitally
Display and text type handwritten by David Clark
Backmatter text set in Triplex by Emigre Graphics
Color separations by Colourscan Print Co Pte Ltd, Singapore
Printed by Imago in China
Production supervision by Brian G. Walker
Designed by Whitney Leader-Picone

Printed in China
(hc) 10 9 8 7 6 5 4 3 2 1

Library of Congress Cataloging-in-Publication Data
Azose, Elana, author
   Never insult a killer zucchini / Elana Azose & Brandon Amancio; illustrated
by David Clark.
     pages cm
 Summary: At a science fair competition, Zucchini is angered by Mr.
Farnsworth's referring to him as lunch, and plots revenge. Includes a section
explaining the scientific terms used in the book.
   ISBN 978-1-58089-618-4 (reinforced for library use)
   ISBN 978-1-60734-827-6 (ebook)
   ISBN 978-1-60734-831-3 (ebook pdf)
1.Inventions—Juvenile fiction. 2. Science fairs—Juvenile fiction.
3. Contests—Juvenile fiction. 4. Zucchini—Juvenile fiction. 5. Humorous
stories. [1. Inventions—Fiction. 2. Science fairs—Fiction. 3. Contests—Fiction.
4. Zucchini—Fiction. 5. Humorous stories.] I. Amancio, Brandon, author.
II. Clark, David, 1960 March 19—illustrator. III. Title.

PZ7.1.A99Ne 2016
[E]—dc23   2014049636

Think the projects in this book are just mad science? Think again! You can actually see, touch, and experience some of them in real life.

ANTIMATTER What do you get when you combine matter with antimatter? Nothing! That's because a particle of matter (such as a hydrogen atom) has the opposite electrical charge as its matching particle of antimatter (anti-hydrogen). When the particles touch, they annihilate each other—both exploding and leaving nothing. Sound scary? Actually, doctors use antimatter to help people. A PET scan (short for positron-emission tomography) sends positrons—a type of antimatter—into a patient's body and shows where they come into contact with certain electrons. The scan helps detect diseases such as cancer. Antimatter can save lives!

BIONIC LIMB People are sometimes born without an arm or a leg, or someone might lose a limb in an accident. Thanks to prosthetics—devices that replace limbs—these people can still enjoy everyday activities. The US military is testing advanced prosthetics to help injured soldiers return to active duty. Advanced prosthetics use microcomputers and have pistons instead of muscles. The mechanical arms and legs can keep moving long after a natural limb would get tired. They really are bionic!

CLONING Have you ever had so much homework that you wished there were two of you? No one has cloned a human, but scientists have cloned quite a few animals for different reasons, including research and medical advancement. Usually, one half of an animal's DNA comes from its mother and the other half from its father. But when Dolly the sheep was born in 1996 in Scotland, all her DNA came from her mother. Dolly was a clone. There have also been cloned monkeys, camels, and even a water buffalo. Pretty weird, huh?

DOOMSDAY DEVICE It'd be impossible to blow up the world (good thing, too!), but special-effects artists can make it seem as if it's been blown up. They work for movie and television studios, creating explosions and other effects. Pyrotechnics are used when fireworks light the sky or rocket ships blast off in the movies. Pyrotechnics also make the *boom!* sound when things explode on-screen. Who knew science was such a big part of showbiz?

ERASER BEAM Tired of hitting the delete key to fix typos? Back when people used typewriters, making a mistake often meant starting over. In 1968 physicist Art Schawlow invented a laser-beam eraser that "zapped" mistakes. The laser's wavelength was set to vaporize the ink and leave the paper intact. Unfortunately, the eraser cost too much to build and sell in stores. But it would've made correcting homework a whole lot more fun, right?

FORCE FIELD Want to travel to the moon for an extended visit? Protection from the harmful radiation caused by solar wind is important for the extra-long space trips planned for the future. Scientists in England worked for years on a deflector shield to block this radiation. They used a magnetic field filled with ionized gas to slow down dangerous particles. But after all that work, it turned out that the best protector in outer space might be . . . plain old plastic! NASA is now working out the details, but it goes to show that everyday objects often save the day.

GIANT ANTS There aren't actual human-sized ants, but there is an insect so huge it can eat a carrot. The giant weta lives in New Zealand and is the largest insect in the world. It looks like a cricket, but it's bigger than a hot-dog bun and way more intimidating.

HYBRID Combining different types of dogs creates new breeds like a Labradoodle (a Labrador retriever and poodle mix) and a miniature schnoxie (a dachshund and miniature schnauzer mix). Breeders don't crossbreed just so they can come up with new funny-sounding names. They're trying to create hybrid puppies with certain desired traits. Believe it or not, there can be hybrids across species, too. A mule is a cross between a donkey and a horse. And how about a cama? It's a cross between a camel and a llama. Ligers are part lion, part tiger. And what's the name of a zebra-donkey hybrid? A zonkey!

INVISIBILITY SUIT Have you ever wanted to be invisible? Scientists at the University of Texas at Dallas have made solid objects invisible—with an on/off switch! They use a sheet of carbon nanotubes, a container of water, and a heater. When they put the nanotubes into the water and heat them up, the nanotubes seem to vanish. When the heat is turned off, the nanotubes reappear. The scientists are controlling the effect of photothermal deflection—that's what causes the mirage on the highway when heat bends light rays to create what looks like a puddle. The scientists say an invisibility cloak could be next.

JET PACK If you had a real-life jet pack, you'd never be late to school again. While scientists haven't been able to make personal jet packs (yet!), a Canadian inventor discovered a way for people to "fly" with a water-shooting jet pack. Put it on like a backpack, get in a large body of water such as a lake, and voilà! A powerful motor pumps a thousand gallons per minute through the system, which thrusts the passenger thirty feet into the air. The jet pack can hover in place, move up or down, or go forward at up to thirty miles per hour. Now if only it would fly above traffic . . .

KILLER ZUCCHINI There might not be actual killer zucchinis lurking in your garden, but carnivorous plants are real. The Venus flytrap is the most famous one, but it isn't the only type of killer plant out there. The pitcher plant has leaves like extra-wide straws that allow it to eat insects and even small animals. Sundew plants use tentacles to surround prey, and bladderworts suck in victims by creating an airtight vacuum. Talk about creepy.

LASER GUN What do you get when you combine a group of engineering students, advanced technology from a Mars rover, and tons of creativity? A real-life laser gun! Students at Seattle University invented a handheld laser gun using laser-induced breakdown spectroscopy. The gun creates a spark, cools down, and lets off light. But instead of being used as a weapon, this laser gun is used to detect harmful substances like lead in paint or toys. Now that's a project that deserves an A!

MIND CONTROL Nobody can actually control your thinking, but have you ever noticed that many fast-food restaurants have red-and-yellow signs? Those aren't random colors. Red can stimulate the body and mind and yellow can stimulate nerves, and together they can make people feel hungry. Color can act on the subconscious mind and influence feelings, which is why a blue room might make someone feel peaceful. So the next time you pass by a fast-food place and crave some fries, figure out if you really do want a snack.

NUCLEAR FUSION Is it hard to force two atoms to squish together and become a single atom? Yup, super hard. The atoms require incredible pressure on them, and it needs to be extremely hot—sometimes over 212 million degrees Farenheit. When nuclear fusion occurs, it creates a lot of energy. Scientists have tried for years to figure out a way to harness the energy to generate clean electricity. Many experiments try to fuse—or stick together—isotopes such as deuterium and tritium. Unfortunately, it takes more energy to fuse them than the reaction produces. And it creates a bunch of super-dangerous particles, too. Now that's one sticky situation.

OUTERQUARIUM If the outside were inside, would it still be the outside? There isn't a whole universe inside its walls, but the Audubon Nature Institute in New Orleans has managed to fit an entire Louisiana swamp inside. There are alligators, a towering cypress tree, and a whole lot of bugs. England is home to the Living Rainforest, a tropical rain forest less than an hour from London. It has more than seven hundred species of tropical plants and animals, including monkeys, snakes, toucans, and a dwarf crocodile. It's like a whole other world—indoors!

PROTOPLASM If you were in a science-fiction movie, you could take a gooey blob of protoplasm (the living part of a cell—nucleus, cytoplasm, and other organelles) and grow new life. Fashion designer Suzanne Lee isn't in a movie, and she doesn't grow henchmen—she uses a gooey blob to grow clothes. She adds sugar to kambucha, a type of fermented tea. Then the bacteria in the kambucha eat the sugar and create a mushy cellulose film. Ms. Lee peels off the film, dries it in the sun, and it turns into homegrown fabric! There's just one small catch: the clothes disintegrate when they get wet.

QUANTUM MECHANICS Ready to boggle your mind? Quantum mechanics is the part of physics that grapples with how particles can be in two places at once and how something could look like it's traveling faster than the speed of light. (Or how a toy could get fixed before it breaks!) Quantum physics also explains how a gecko can walk across a ceiling and not fall off. Some animals use claws or suction cups on their feet, but thanks to the Casimir effect (also called "sticky quantum force"), the gecko is attracted to the ceiling like a magnet. Millions of microscopic hairs on a gecko's feet create fluctuations in the energy field in the empty space between the hairs and the ceiling, making its feet "stick." Now if only that worked on human feet . . .

RADIOACTIVE GERBIL Gerbils are definitely cute pets, but a radioactive one might not be so much fun. Radioactive atoms aren't very stable, and they decay and break apart in tiny explosions. These explosions cause small particles to fly off every which way, creating radiation. The process gives off light, which makes radioactive elements look like they're glowing. Too much exposure to radiation can be harmful, but controlled doses can save lives. X-rays use radiation to help doctors see inside the human body, and radiation therapy can help treat cancer. You might say that radiation gets a glowing report!

SHRINK RAY All those quarters getting heavy in your pocket? Scientists at Florida's National High Magnetic Field Laboratory (aka the Mag Lab) can shrink a quarter to the size of a dime—in a millionth of a second! The lab's high-voltage shrinking machine sends a million amps of electricity (enough to power a thousand houses) through a copper coil wrapped around a quarter. There's a giant flash of light, and the coil explodes! The quarter stays in one piece, but something called the Lorentz force pushes its particles inward, causing it to smoosh down to dime size. Talk about shrinking funds. . . .

TELEPORTER What if you were floating around in outer space and got a craving for pizza? You couldn't exactly order a teleport delivery of an extra-large with onions. Or could you? NASA is preparing to use 3-D printers to print out food for astronauts in space. This type of printer adds layers on top of layers on top of layers, until a 3-D object is created. In order to replicate a pizza, the printer uses powdered nutrients, mixes them with oil and water, and prints until the pizza is "cooked." Bon appétit?

UNDERWATER LAIR It's true—people can live under water and not just in a submarine. There's an underwater lab in Florida called Aquarius that ocean researchers can visit for up to ten days at a time. There are six bunks, a bathroom with a shower, a refrigerator, and a microwave. It even has computers and air-conditioning. Who's ready for an underwater adventure—complete with email?

VORTEX In science-fiction stories vortexes make things disappear or allow time travel. A well-known vortex is the Bermuda Triangle, where many ships have supposedly vanished. Some people believe in another type of vortex—healing vortexes. The ones in Sedona, Arizona, are believed to have beneficial energy that comes up from the earth. Lots of people go to Sedona every year to visit them. There are maps, guides, and even special tours to find these unique spots. Let the healing begin!

WEATHER MACHINE Want to go skiing in the summertime? There are machines that can make snow on ski trails when it's near freezing, but what about machines to make it snow when it's a hundred degrees outside? They really exist, and indoor ski resorts are popping up around the globe. Even though it might be sizzling outside, inside it's frosty (and snowy!). When it's time to make snow at the United Arab Emirates' ski resort, blast coolers bring the temperature down to about seventeen degrees Farenheit. Then they send gallons of cold water through snow guns in the ceiling. When the water is blown into the freezing air, it crystallizes and forms real snow. Brrrr . . .

X-RAY GLASS Ever wished you could see through walls? What about seeing through someone's skin? Scientists in Idaho have developed three types of glasses to help medical professionals see under skin. One type of glasses makes it easier to find blood oxygenation or concentration. Doctors and nurses can use another type to find hidden veins, and yet another to discover internal bruises they might never have known about otherwise. It's almost like having superhero vision.

YOUTH SERUM Although kids often wish they could grow up faster, grown-ups sometimes want to feel younger. Well, scientists at Harvard think they might have found a compound that slows down aging. Overweight mice that were given a drug called reservatrol were able to run twice as far as mice that weren't overweight, and they lived 15 percent longer. It sounds pretty amazing, but a lot of tests still need to be done to make sure it's safe for humans to take. An anti-aging drug that caused problems would be just what the doctor *didn't* order. . . .

ZERO GRAVITY You don't have to travel to outer space to float like an astronaut. The lifting, weightless sensation riders feel on a speeding roller coaster is called free fall, and it's similar to what astronauts feel in orbit. There are even special airplane flights where the pilot makes shapes in the air called parabolas. When the plane is tilted upward, passengers feel heavy and are pushed toward the floor. But when the plane levels off and enters free fall, riders get to feel simulated zero gravity. People on board can float, bounce, fly, twirl, and somersault in the air, just like astronauts in space. What are you waiting for?